From The Women's Press Ltd
124 Shoreditch High Street, London E1

FEMINIST LIBRARY
Hungerford House
Victoria Embankment
London WC2N 6PA
01-930-0715

Angela Martin lives in Manchester, and trained as a textile designer. She works on the North Manchester Women's Health Project and has contributed cartoons and drawings locally for the past two years.

A Good Bitch is the first published collection of Angela Martin's work.

A GOOD BITCH

Cartoons by
Angela Martin

 The Women's Press

Seasonal work
Long hours, low pay,
no "Health and safety"
no danger money . . . . . .
. . . . They said
I could keep the dress. . . .

First published by The Women's Press Limited 1984
A member of the Namara Group
124 Shoreditch High Street, London E1 6JE

Copyright © Angela Martin 1984

British Library Cataloguing in Publication Data

Martin, Angela
  A Good Bitch.
  1. English wit and humour, Pictorial
  I. Title
  741.5'942   NC1479

  ISBN 0-7043-3956-0

Printed and bound in Great Britain
by Mackays of Chatham Limited, Kent

Acknowledgements

Thanks to Dale, Brenda, North Manchester Women's
Health Project (Steph, Jane, Maggie, Gail, Judith and Di)
and Suzanne and The Women's Press.

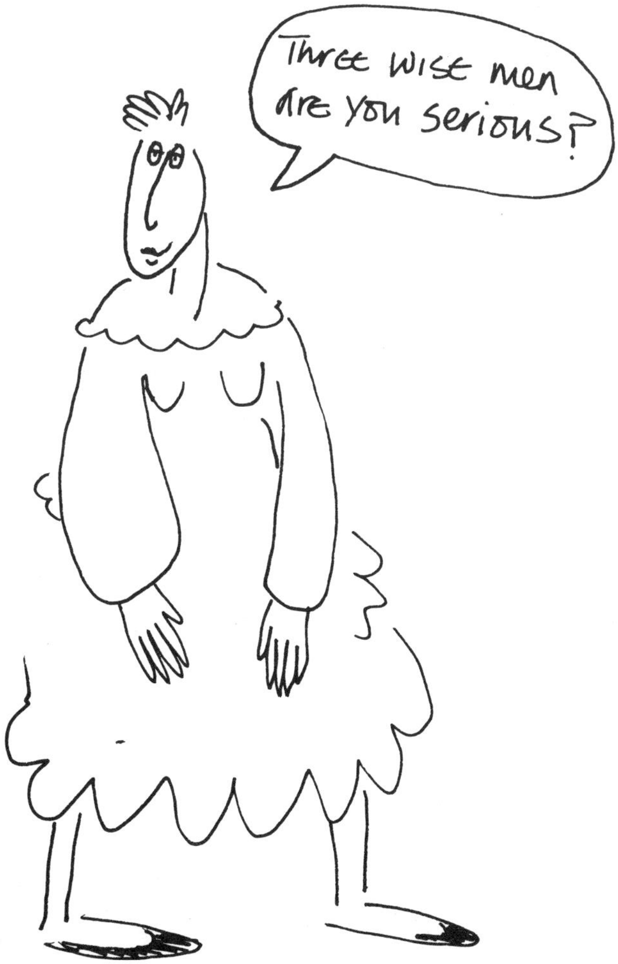
Three wise men
are you serious?

I think I am a
good bloke
therefore I am
a good bloke....

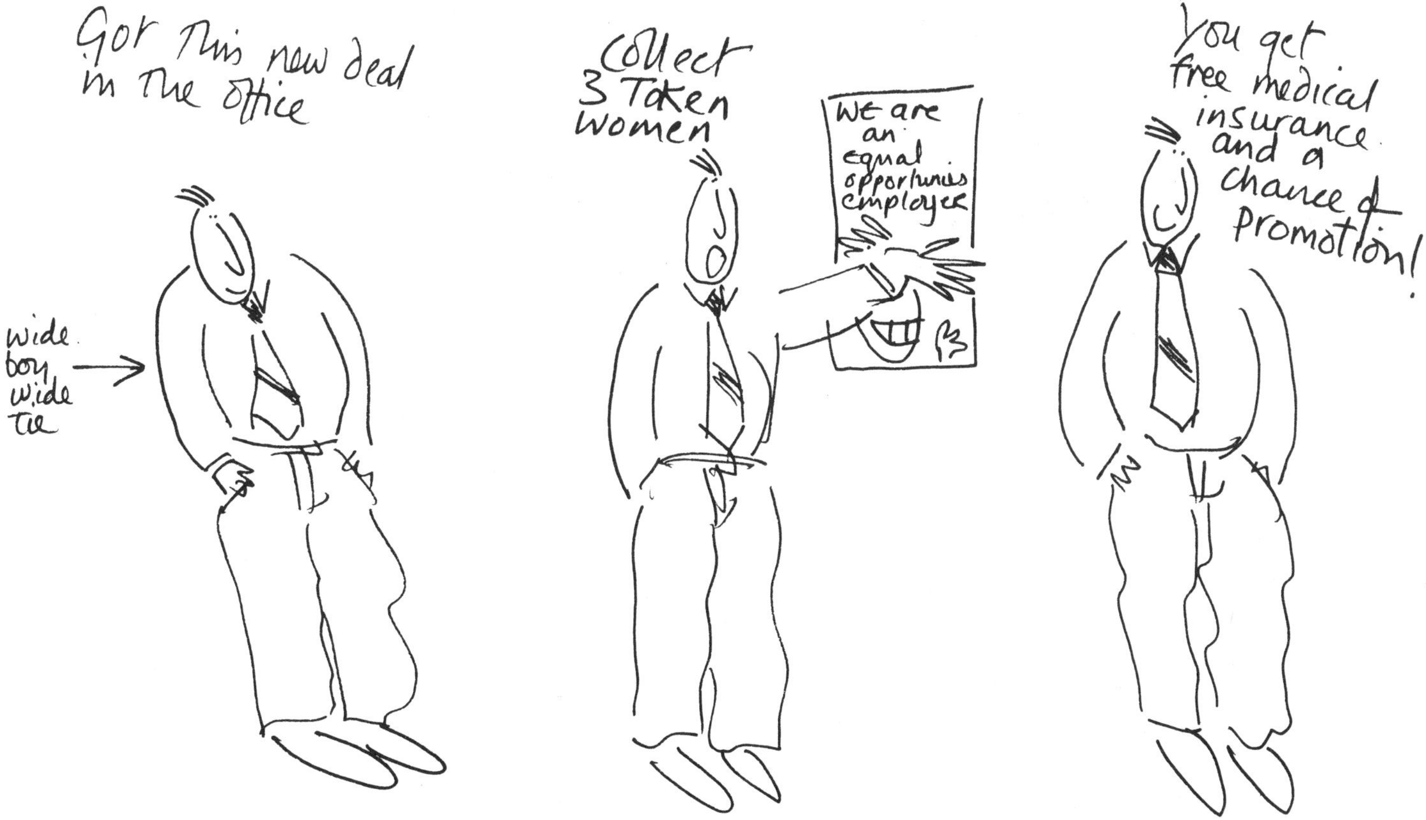
Got this new deal in the office
wide boy wide tie
Collect 3 token women
We are an equal opportunities employer
You get free medical insurance and a chance of promotion!

Compromise N° 732,569,031
Frilly dress and hairy legs
He didn't even notice

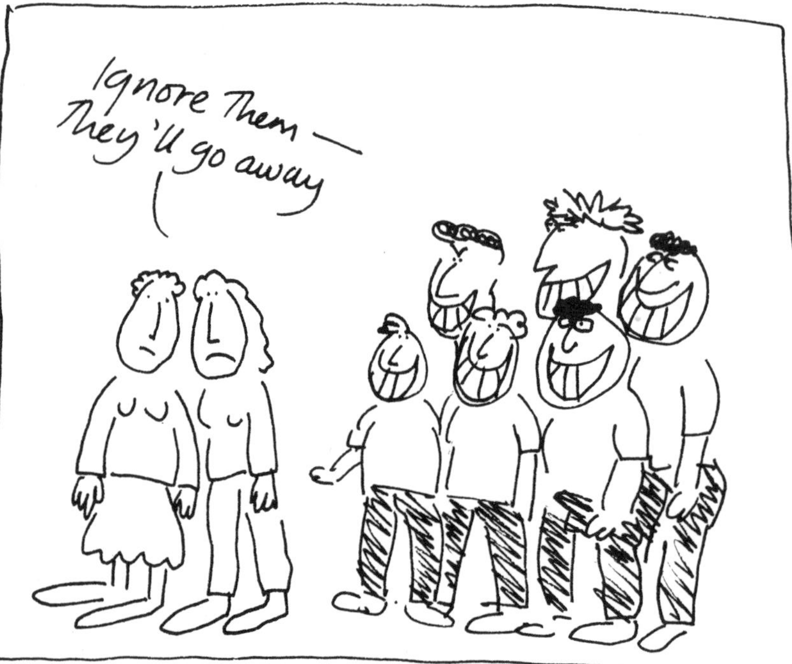

But WILL they?
same place, same time
NEXT CENTURY.....

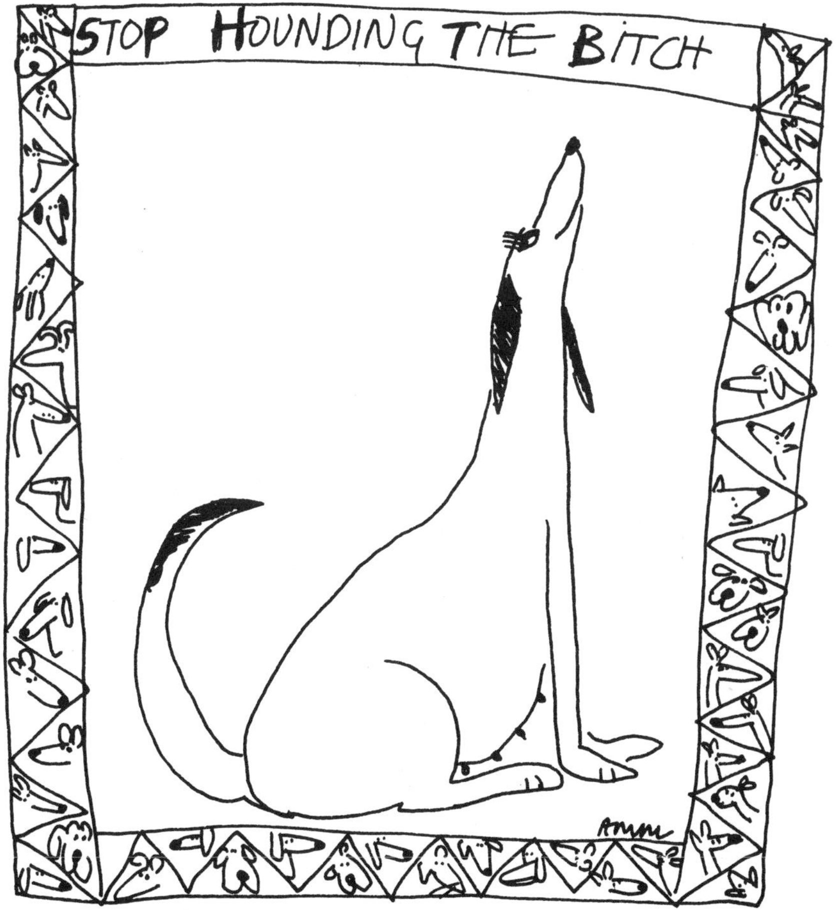
STOP HOUNDING THE BITCH
Annie

I come home —
after a hard day's
WORK —
The least I can expect is
a hot MEAL!
MOTHER HUBBARD'S CUPBOARD

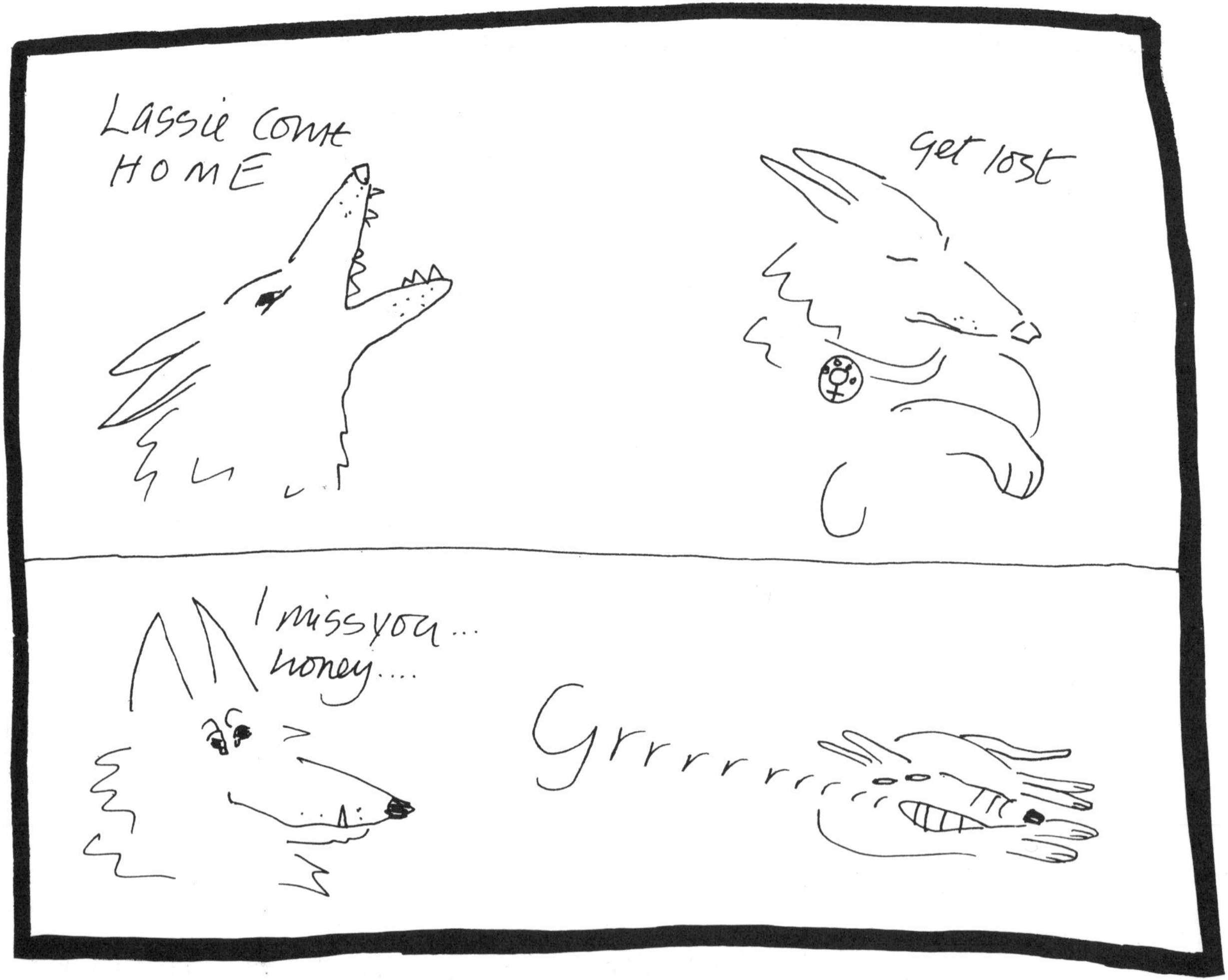
Lassie come HOME
get lost
I miss you... honey....
Grrrrrrrr

timber

COMPROMISE Nº 76711874/AZ
SENSIBLE KIT
betrayed only
by a PINK
DESIGNER KNAPSACK
WITH GOLD TRIMMINGS
It's my sister's

I suppose you're going to mention sexual harassment...

yes

Pity. Why pick on me? I'm on your side.

You feminists make yourselves so unattractive to men, you know

Especially such a lovely young ladies as yourselves......

I don't care what
your name is———
I want to speak to
the answering
machine ......

The Temp ......

This is boring
ZZZ
I'm not going to last
yawn
hate figures hate calculators hate
oh no
1st Day? you'll get used to it — after a while
I doubt it.....
bored sigh
Fed up — 3 hours to lunch..
cheer up — it might never happen!
ugh
I wonder what he looks like without any clothes on....

MARITAL ARTS
COURSE: BEGINNERS
Morning darling
whoops my foot slipped
tea?

COMPROMISE N° 788612|B|AZ1
Clothes, jumble
Sale, shoes oxfam
Hair, ~~bread~~ knife
Bike : DIOR

I now declare you
whole person and
whole servicing
person....

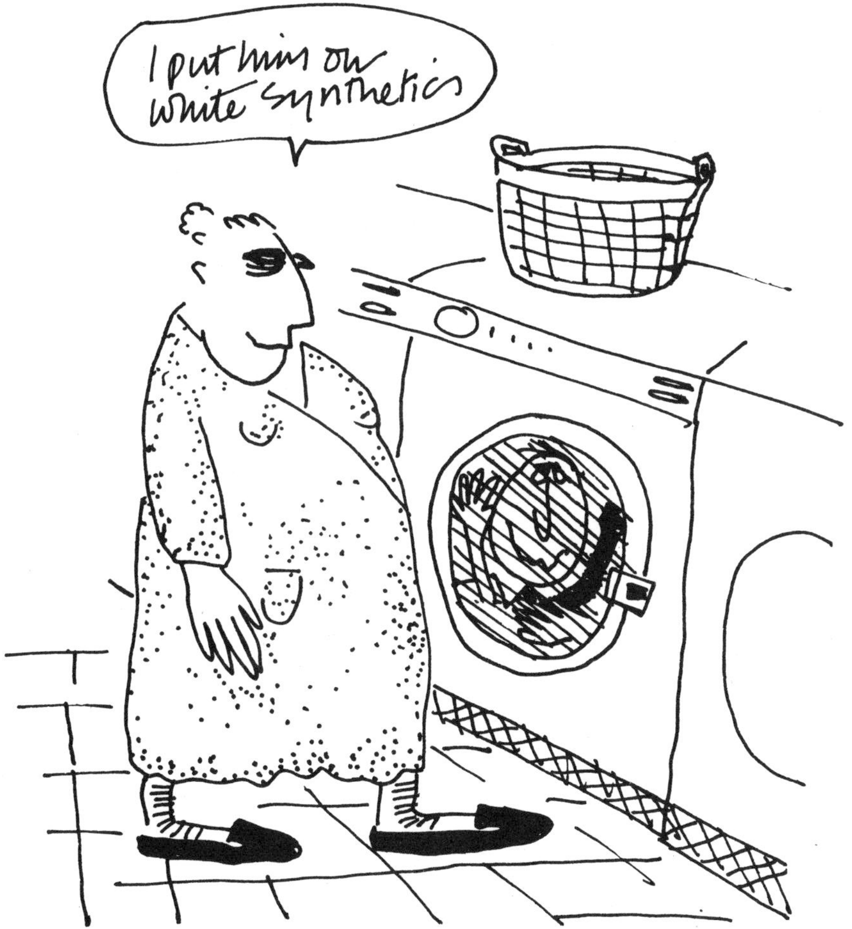
I put him on white synthetics

THE PILL WAS SO <u>BORING</u>

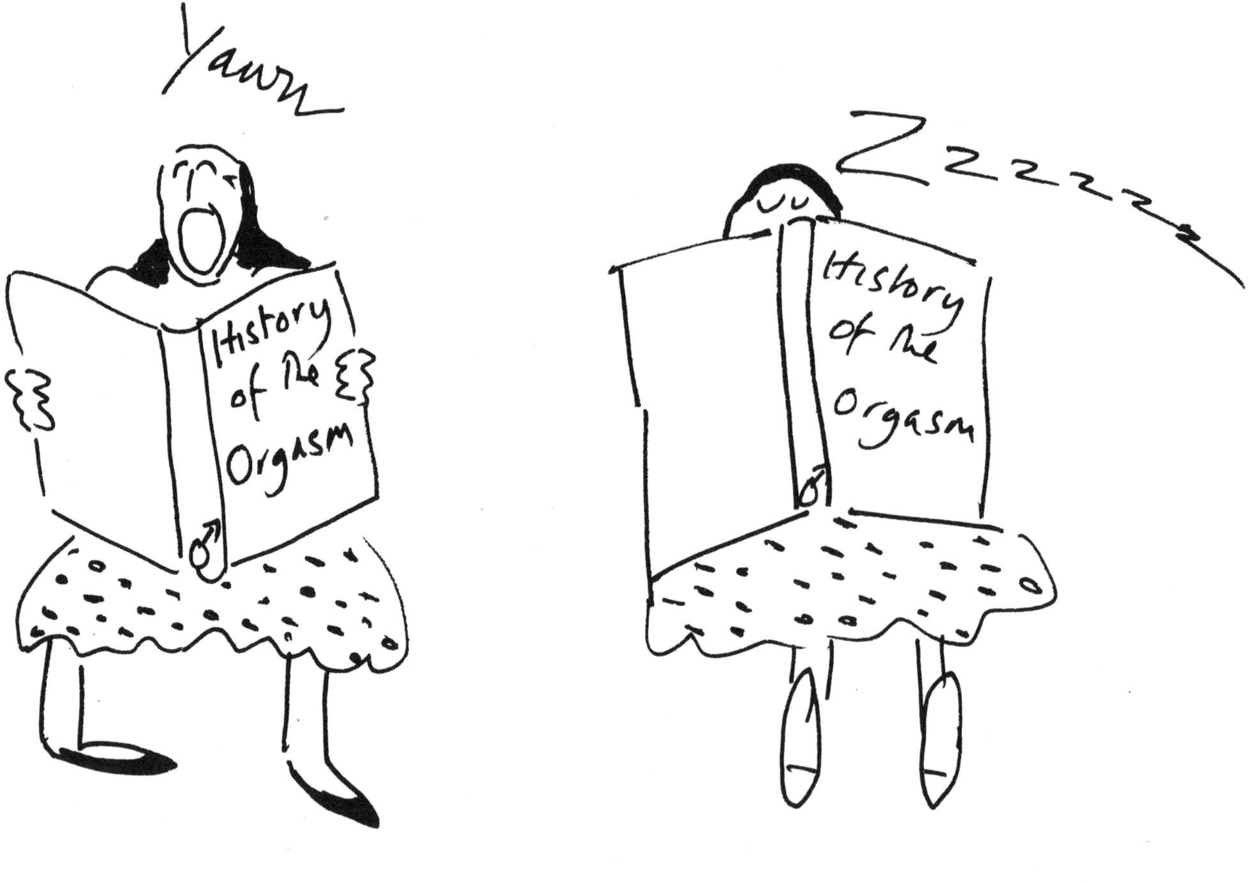
Yawn
History of the Orgasm
Zzzzzz
History of the Orgasm

FRIDGE ANALYSIS

discover you friends'
true characters— Just look inside
their fridges
"More acurate Than horoscopes"
Psychic News.

Case study ①

cat food

dripping

milk

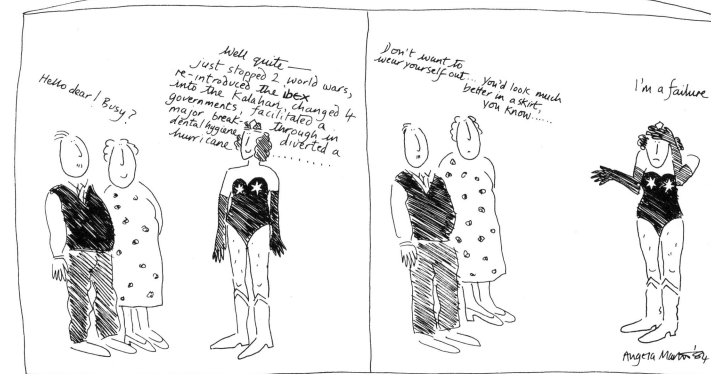

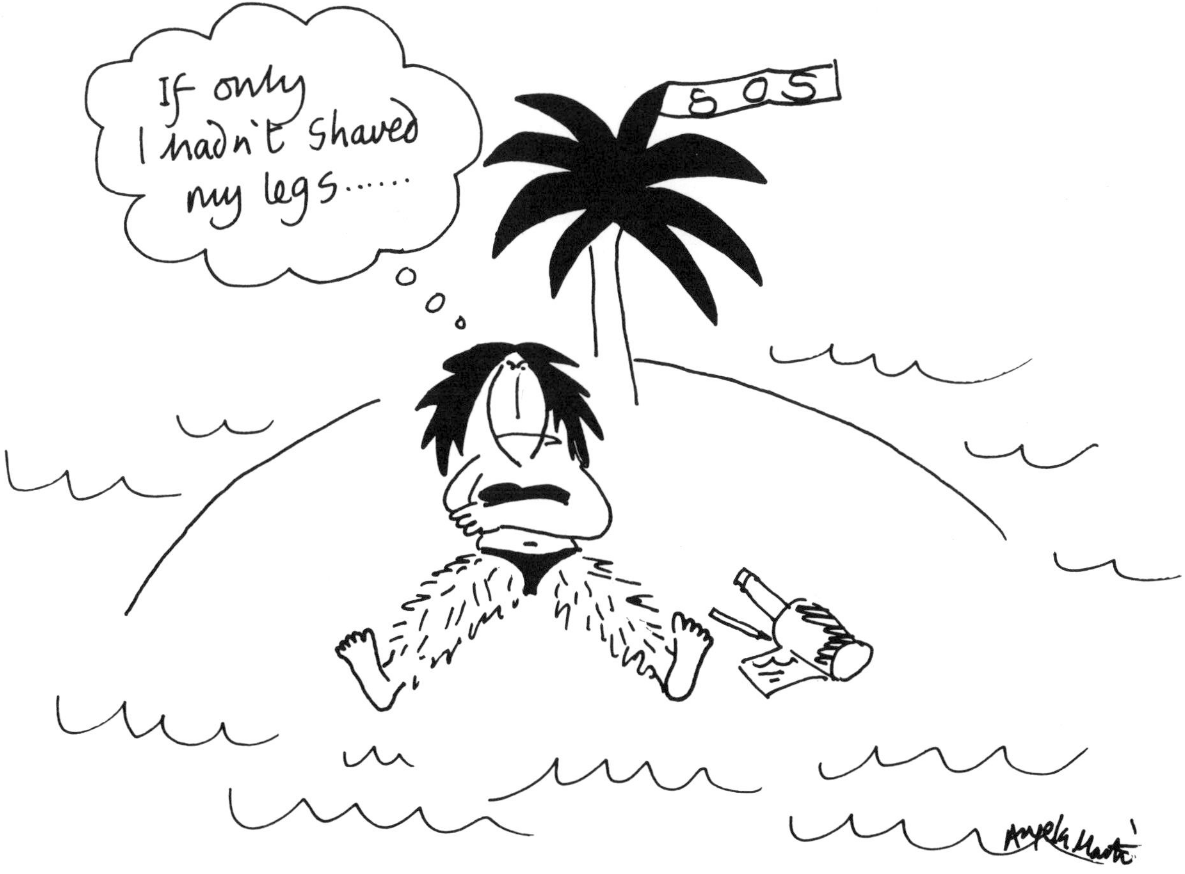

If only I hadn't shaved my legs......
SOS

A hot flush?
RELAX
activate – water jets
fans and ice bags.....
RELAX
Really cool!...
RELAX

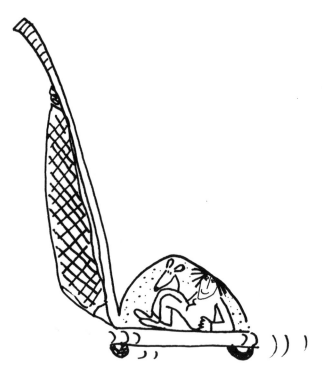

brought up in a vaccum . . . .

Wonder Woman Wips out to corner shop, having forgotten cat food
Bloody cat

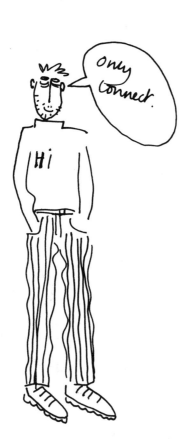

Shouldn't This book be vetted by an anti-sexist male?
has the anti-sexist male been vetted?
Angela Martin